WONDER BOOKS®

It Is Friday

The Sound of FR

By Cynthia Klingel and Robert B. Noyed

The
**Child's
World®**

Friday is a fun day.

I never frown on Friday.

On Friday, I run home from school.

On Friday, I play with my friend.

On Friday, I eat french fries.

On Friday, I catch a frog.

On Friday, I buy fresh fruit.

On Friday, I sit on my front porch.

On Friday, I get a gift from Aunt Fran.

Friday is the best day of the week.

Word List

Fran	frog
french fries	from
fresh	front
Friday	frown
friend	fruit

Note to Parents and Educators

Welcome to Wonder Books® Phonics Readers! These books are based on current research that supports the idea that our brains detect patterns rather than apply rules. This means that children learn to read more easily when they are taught the familiar spelling patterns found in English. As children progress in their reading, they can use these spelling patterns to figure out more complex words.

The Phonics Readers texts provide the opportunity to practice and apply knowledge of the sounds in natural language. The ten books on the long and short vowels introduce the sounds using familiar onsets and *rimes*, or spelling patterns, for reinforcement. The letter(s) before the vowel in a word are considered the onset. Changing the onset allows the consonant books in the series to maintain the practice and reinforcement of the rimes. The repeated use of a word or phrase reinforces the target sound. The twenty-one consonants and eight blends ("ch," "br," etc.) also use the onset-and-rimes technique.

As an example, the word "cat" might be used to present the short "a" sound, with the letter "c" being the onset and "–at" being the rime. This approach provides practice and reinforcement for the short "a" sound, since there are many familiar words with the "–at" rime.

The number on the spine of each book facilitates arranging the books in the order in which the sounds are learned. The books can also be arranged into groups of long vowels, short vowels, consonants, and blends. All the books in each grouping have their numbers printed in the same color on the spine. The books can be grouped and regrouped easily and quickly, depending on the teacher's needs.

The stories and accompanying photographs in this series are based on time-honored concepts in children's literature: Well-written, engaging texts and colorful, high-quality photographs combine to produce books that children want to read again and again.

Dr. Peg Ballard
Minnesota State University, Mankato, MN

About the Authors

Cynthia Klingel has worked as a high school English teacher and an elementary school teacher. She is currently the curriculum director for a Minnesota school district. Cynthia lives with her family in Mankato, Minnesota.

Robert B. Noyed started his career as a newspaper reporter. Since then, he has worked in school communications and public relations at the state and national level. Robert lives with his family in Brooklyn Center, Minnesota.

Published by The Child's World®

PO Box 326
Chanhassen, MN 55317-0326
800-599-READ
www.childsworld.com

With special thanks to the Asencio, Bernal, and Robles families
for supplying the modeling for this book.

Photo Credits
© Siede Preis/PhotoDisc: 13
All other photos © Romie Flanagan

Project Coordination: Editorial Directions, Inc.
Photo Research: Alice K. Flanagan

Library of Congress Cataloging-in-Publication Data
Klingel, Cynthia Fitterer.
  It is Friday : the sound of "fr" / by Cynthia Klingel and Robert B. Noyed.
      p. cm. — (Wonder books. A phonics reader)
  Summary: Simple text about a special day of the week and repetition of
the "fr" blend help readers learn this sound.
  ISBN 1-56766-051-7 (Library Bound : alk. paper)
  [1. Days—Fiction. 2. Alphabet.] I. Noyed, Robert B. II. Title. III. Wonder books (Chanhassen, Minn.). Phonics.
  PZ7.K6798 It 2002
  [E]—dc21
                              2002001001